THOSE CAN-DO PIGS

SOME PIGS I KNOW ARE CALLED CAN-DO'S
(YOU MIGHT HAVE SEEN THEM ON THE NEWS).
THEY ARE BOLD AND BRAVE AND TRUE,
AND THERE IS NOTHING THEY CAN'T DO....

DUTTON CHILDREN'S BOOKS
NEW YORK

For Neddy Ballgame and family—
Judy, Phoebe, and Gus

CIP Data is available.

Published in the United States 1996
by Dutton Children's Books,
a division of Penguin Books USA Inc.
375 Hudson Street, New York, New York 10014
Designed by Barbara Powderly
Printed in Hong Kong
First Edition   10 9 8 7 6 5 4 3 2 1
ISBN 0-525-45495-0

The line about beating the bongos was inspired
by a song by the British rock group Dire Straits.

In the morning, bright and early,
Can-Do Pigs are gruff and surly
Till they've had their toast and tea—
Then they're happy as can be.

Before a Can-Do Pig steps out,
He takes a bath and scrubs his snout.
He shines his shoes and ties his tie,
Then gives his mom a kiss good-bye.

Can-Do Pigs can take a ride
Up and down the countryside.
They stop at Vern's to change a tire
And fix the fan belt with some wire.

When Can-Do Pigs are building roads,
They get some help from frogs and toads.
They rake the dirt and hose it down,
Then all jump in and roll around.

Those Can-Do Pigs can do repairs,
Mending tables, lamps, and chairs.
They try to make them good as new
With a hammer, nails, and glue.

Those pigs can do most anything.
Have you ever heard them sing?
Or play piano with a stick?
Or beat them bongos with a brick?

A Can-Do Pig could can-can well—
Until the day she tripped and fell
Down the stairs and out the door.
(She doesn't can-can anymore.)

In the summer when it's hot,
Can-Do Pigs don't do a lot.
They rub themselves with suntan lotion,
Then jump into the salty ocean.

Can-Do Pigs in pink pajamas
Can row a boat to the Bahamas.
If a hungry shark attacks,
Those piggies give him forty whacks.

In the grass down by the shore,
A Can-Do Pig disturbs a boa—
The snake wakes up and starts to hiss,
Then gives that pig a great big kiss.

Can-Do Pigs can never lie.
They just can't—I don't know why.
George Washingpig chopped down a tree,
Then told his father, "It was me!"

Can-Do Pigs can climb up trees.
They hang from branches by their knees.
Don't worry if you see one fall,
He'll bounce right back—*boing!*—like a ball.

Those pigs can fly—did you know that?
Just like a bee, a bird, a bat.
You can see them in the sky.
Watch out—duck! One just flew by.

From the closet down the hall
Steps a pig who's very small.
He smiles and asks, "How do you do?"
"Quite well," I say, "but who are you?"

"I'm Super-Dooper Can-Do Pig,
And though it's true I'm not that big,
There's not a thing that I can't do.
Just watch! I'll clean your house for you."

He lifts me up into the air,
And then he mops beneath my chair.
Next we fly around the room
While he sweeps it with a broom.

He cleans each cranny—every nook,
And blows the dust off every book,
And when he's done, he flies away.
"I'll be back," he calls, "someday...."

Pigs can rocket to the moon.
They leave at ten, arrive by noon.
They stop for lunch out there in space
At some little fast-food place.

TAKE OUT

At the rodeo, Can-Do's rule,
Dressed in outfits that are cool.
They can ride those bulls so well.
(I've never heard of one that fell.)

Can-Do Piggies can't stand WAR.
They stamp their feet and shout, "NO MORE!"
They put the generals in a pile,
Then they tickle them awhile.

In the winter, when it snows,
And that chilly north wind blows,
Those pigs can build a giant hog.
(For the nose they use a log.)

Those pigs can coast down any hill.
(The steepest gives the biggest thrill.)
And if some piggies don't have sleds,
They don't mind—they use their beds.

It's your birthday! What? No cake?
Someone's made a big mistake.
Ask those pigs to bake one quick.
White or chocolate, take your pick.

Do your cellar stairs go *creak*?
Perhaps you'd better take a peek.
But bring along a Can-Do Pig.
(Make sure you find one that is big.)

Can-Do Pigs are quite amazing.
I've seen them late at night, stargazing—
Stretched out on their bristly backs,
Munching on their midnight snacks.

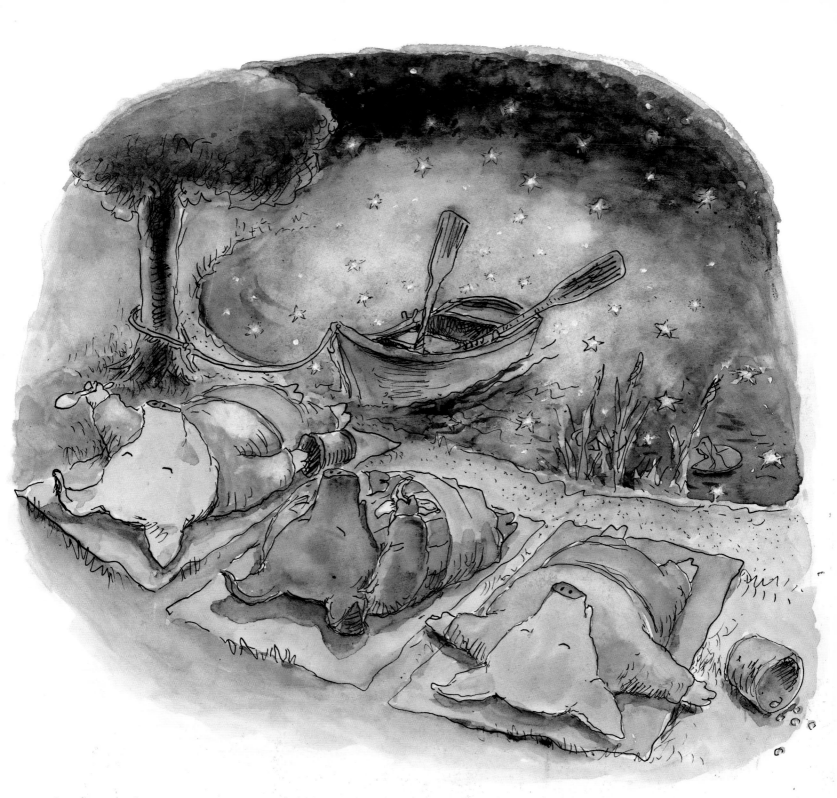

Lying there beside the lake,
Are those piggies still awake?
I listen closely — not one peep.
Those Can-Do Pigs are sound asleep.

It's good to have a Can-Do friend
To stand beside you till the end.
No matter where, no matter when,
It's good to have a Can-Do friend.

j P   9-96
McPhail, David

Those can-do pigs

w/P